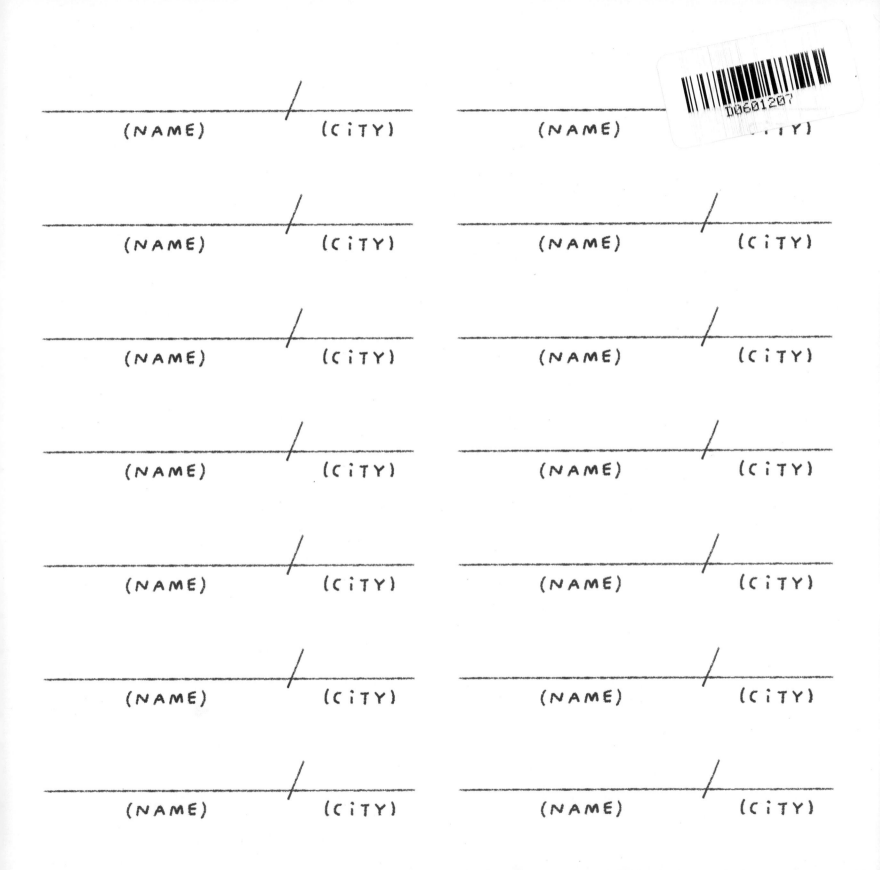

(NAME) / (CiTY)   (NAME) / (CiTY)

(NAME) / (CiTY)   (NAME) / (CiTY)

(NAME) / (CiTY)   (NAME) / (CiTY)

(NAME) / (CiTY)   (NAME) / (CiTY)

(NAME) / (CiTY)   (NAME) / (CiTY)

(NAME) / (CiTY)   (NAME) / (CiTY)

(NAME) / (CiTY)   (NAME) / (CiTY)

GIVE THIS BOOK AWAY!

(Unless it came from
your local library, in which case,
share it with a friend before
you check it back in.)

For Juan Carlos, one of the most
giving people I know. Abrazos! —D.F.

For the libraries and librarians,
who give to the community —M.T.

THIS IS A BORZOI BOOK PUBLISHED BY ALFRED A. KNOPF

Text copyright © 2022 by Darren Farrell
Jacket art and interior illustrations copyright © 2022 by Maya Tatsukawa

All rights reserved. Published in the United States by Alfred A. Knopf,
an imprint of Random House Children's Books, a division of
Penguin Random House LLC, New York.

Knopf, Borzoi Books, and the colophon are registered trademarks of
Penguin Random House LLC.

Visit us on the Web! rhcbooks.com

Educators and librarians, for a variety of teaching tools,
visit us at RHTeachersLibrarians.com

Library of Congress Cataloging-in-Publication Data is available upon request.
ISBN 978-0-593-48051-9 (trade) — ISBN 978-0-593-48052-6 (lib. bdg.) —
ISBN 978-0-593-48053-3 (ebook)

The text of this book is set in 21-point Brandon Text Medium.
The illustrations were created digitally with handmade textures and stamps.
Book design by Taline Boghosian

MANUFACTURED IN CHINA

October 2022   10 9 8 7 6 5 4 3 2 1   First Edition

GIVE THIS BOOK AWAY!

written by
Darren Farrell

illustrated by
Maya Tatsukawa

Alfred A. Knopf 🐎 New York

You know, a little bit of **LOVE** can go a long way.

Don't believe it?

See for yourself.

After you've read
all the words and
admired all the pictures,

when you've
asked every ask

and thought
every think,

take this book
and give it away.

Seriously,
find someone you've
NEVER talked to
before. And hand them
THiS book.

How about a new face on the playground?

Or someone at the grocery store?

Or a person sitting all alone?

No matter who you choose,
giving is an act of **LOVE.**

So, even though you may be
worried and you might feel
a little bit uncomfortable—

WATCH WHAT HAPPENS!

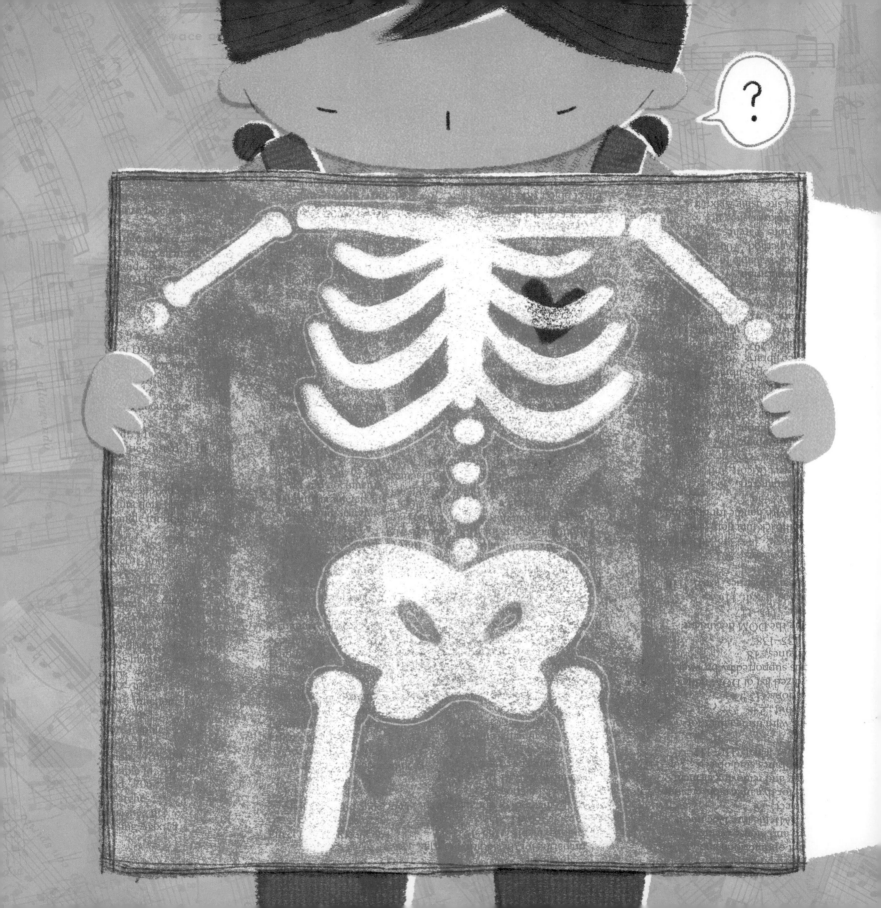

Something thunderous
stirs inside you when you
give good things away.

Pay attention
to the fireworks.

They start in your
chest and spread
to your smile.

And before you know it,
they will electrify your whole body

and charge the air all around you with invisible particles of JOY!

Get ready!
You've almost reached the important page.

The one you've got to hold up
when you give this book away.

THIS IS IT!
It's now or never!

Now stand back. Nobody knows what will happen next.

There could be giggles. There might be hugs (ask first!).

Perhaps, if nobody has done a nice thing
for your person in a long, long time,
they might even cry.

Do you know what? *You* might cry, too!

WOW! Look at what you can do
with just one little book.

So please don't stop there.
Keep going!

Give your
words.

Give your
hands.

Give your
smiles.

Give your
time.

Give your
food.

GIVE
YOUR
ALL.

Who knows?
Maybe one day,
someone will give
this book . . .

the one you are
holding in your
hands right now . . .

the one you are about
to give away . . .

back to you.

Then you can see all the places
this little book of love has been.

But first,

don't forget to . . .

GIVE
THIS
BOOK
AWAY!

THIS
IS
FOR
YOU!

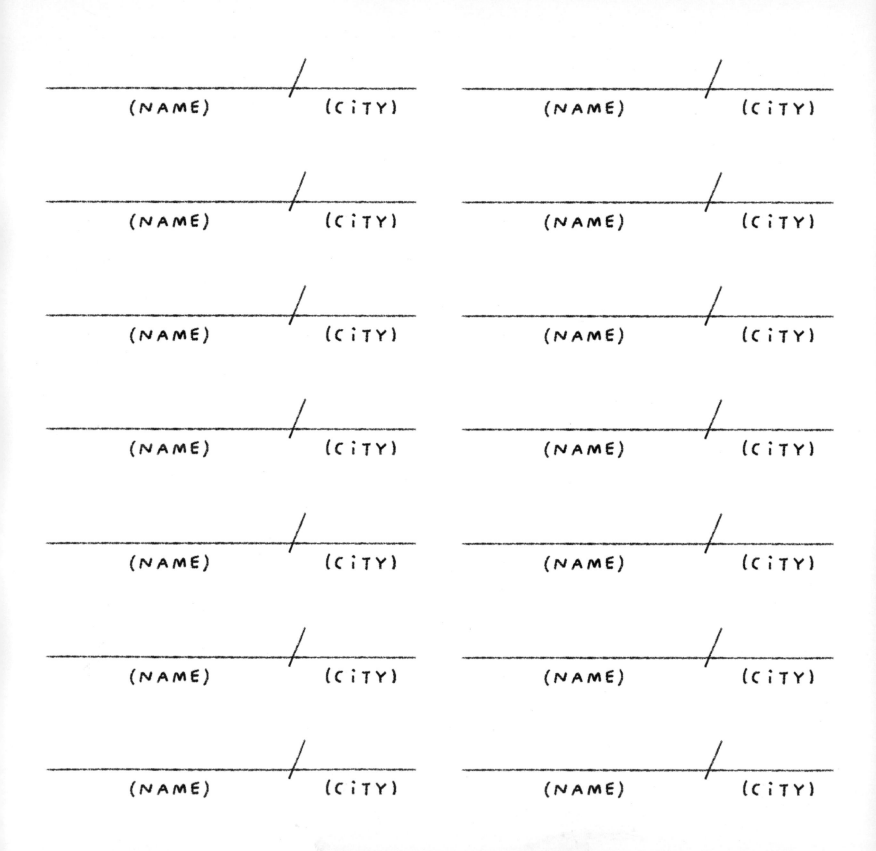